Oh No, Gotta Go #2

Susan Middleton Elya   pictures by **Lynne Avril**

G. P. Putnam's Sons

To Audrey's girls: Camille, Marlee, and Karyn. —S.M.E.

For Brian—You're #1! —L.A.

G. P. PUTNAM'S SONS
A division of Penguin Young Readers Group.
Published by The Penguin Group.
Penguin Group (USA) Inc., 375 Hudson Street, New York, NY 10014, U.S.A.
Penguin Group (Canada), 90 Eglinton Avenue East, Suite 700, Toronto, Ontario, Canada M4P 2Y3
(a division of Pearson Penguin Canada Inc.).
Penguin Books Ltd, 80 Strand, London WC2R 0RL, England.
Penguin Ireland, 25 St. Stephen's Green, Dublin 2, Ireland (a division of Penguin Books Ltd.).
Penguin Group (Australia), 250 Camberwell Road, Camberwell, Victoria 3124, Australia
(a division of Pearson Australia Group Pty Ltd).
Penguin Books India Pvt Ltd, 11 Community Centre, Panchsheel Park, New Delhi - 110 017, India.
Penguin Group (NZ), Cnr Airborne and Rosedale Roads, Albany, Auckland 1310, New Zealand
(a division of Pearson New Zealand Ltd).
Penguin Books (South Africa) (Pty) Ltd, 24 Sturdee Avenue, Rosebank, Johannesburg 2196, South Africa.
Penguin Books Ltd, Registered Offices: 80 Strand, London WC2R 0RL, England.

Manufactured in China by South China Printing Co. Ltd.
Design by Katrina Damkoehler. Text set in Symphony.
The art was done in chalk pastels with acrylic medium on Arches watercolor paper.

Library of Congress Cataloging-in-Publication Data
Elya, Susan Middleton, 1955– Oh no, gotta go #2 / Susan Middleton Elya ; illustrated by Lynne Avril. p. cm.
Summary: On her way back from a picnic with her parents, a little girl who did not need to "tinkle"
suddenly remembers that there is more than one reason to visit a restroom.
Text includes some Spanish words and phrases. [1. Defecation—Fiction. 2. Picnicking—Fiction.
3. Spanish language—Fiction. 4. Stories in rhyme.] I. Avril, Lynne, 1951– ill. II. Title.
III. Title: Oh no, gotta go number two.   PZ8.3.E514Oha 2007   [E]—dc22   2006009156

ISBN 978-0-399-24308-0
1 3 5 7 9 10 8 6 4 2
First Impression

Glossary

accidente (ahk see DEHN teh) accident

adiós (ah DYOCE) good-bye

agua (AH gwah) water

ándale (AHN dah leh) hurry up

ay (EYE) hey

basura (bah SOO rah) trash

caca (KAH kah) poop

casa (KAH sah) house

deliciosa (deh lee SYOE sah) delicious

detalle (deh TAH yeh) detail

dónde está (DOHN deh ehs TAH) where is it

espinaca (ehs pee NAH kah) spinach

hija (EE hah) daughter

jugo (HOO goe) juice

limonada (lee moe NAH dah) lemonade

la calle (LAH KAH yeh) street

las llaves (LAHS YAH vehs) keys

la puerta (LAH PWEHR tah) door

la tienda (LAH TYEHN dah) store

madre (MAH dreh) mother

Mamá (mah MAH) Mom

merienda (meh ree EHN dah) picnic

mi (MEE) my

nada (NAH dah) not anything

ojos (OE hoce) eyes

padre (PAH dreh) father

Papá (pah PAH) Dad

rápidamente (rrah pee dah MEHN teh) rapidly

sabrosa (sah BROE sah) tasty

sí (SEE) yes

un baño (OON BAH nyoe) a bathroom

y tú (EE TOO) and you

My parents and I were out walking **la calle**.
Mamá packed a basket with every **detalle**.

I sat on my trike and was ready to roam.

I'd gone to the **baño** before we left home.

Papá bought the food at the store—**la tienda**,
to bring to the park for a nice **merienda**.

Mamá put our blanket down under a tree
and set out the stuff for a picnic for three.

"You've had a long bike ride," said **mi papá**.
"Do you need **un baño**?" asked **mi mamá**.

"No!" I assured them, shaking my head.
I hadn't drunk anything. I'd planned ahead.

We feasted on salad, tasty—**sabrosa**.
Mamá called it spinach. **¡Deliciosa!**

Papá stretched his legs,
and he finished his wine.

Papá helped me swing while **Mamá** packed the basket.
Then right before leaving, I knew he would ask it.

"No! I don't need to." I went to my trike,
hopped on and pedaled. "You go if you'd like."

Papá shook his head, said, "Let's go find your **madre**."
"Everyone ready?" **Mamá** asked **mi padre**.

We tossed our **basura**, said bye to the park,
and headed for our place
before it got dark.

Meanwhile, my insides were gurgling and grumbling.
I wasn't hungry, but something was rumbling.

Mamá and **Papá** were in deep conversation.
I pedaled along with that funny sensation.

I didn't drink **jugo** or pink **limonada**.
I didn't drink **agua**. I didn't drink **nada**!

But then I remembered the thing I forgot.

There's more than one reason
to sit on the pot.

Mamá put her hands on her hips, turned to Dad.

The look in her **ojos** showed she was mad.

"Didn't you ask her if she had to go?"

"**¡Sí!**" he insisted. "Your daughter said no!"

"**¡Ay!**" said **Mamá**. "She had nothing to drink."

She looked at my face. It was wrinkly and pink.

"**¡Hija!**" she said, as **Mamá** got an inkling
that this was the big kind of going, not tinkling.

"The salad!

The spinach!

The green **espinaca!**"

"Why, that means," **Papá** said, "she has to go **caca!**"

"¡Ándale, hija!" So I pedaled faster.
If I didn't hurry, there'd be a disaster!

Papá scooped me up and he ran for our place.
Mamá grabbed the trike, look of pain on her face.

The park was way back and our **casa**—so far.
I wished in that moment we'd driven our car!

We rounded our street corner. "**¡Rápidamente!**
Hurry, **Papá**, so there's no **accidente!**"

Mamá tossed the keys but **Papá** missed his chance.
"**¡Las llaves!**" she hollered. I started to dance.

He opened **la puerta**, and I rushed inside,
went straight to the **baño**, so happy, I cried.

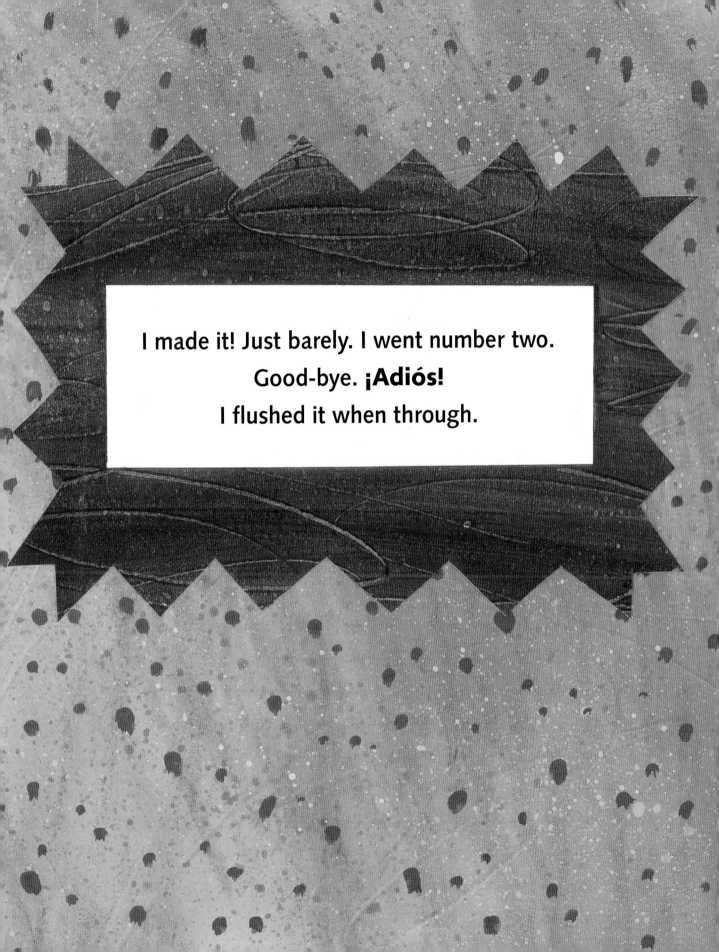

I made it! Just barely. I went number two.
Good-bye. **¡Adiós!**
I flushed it when through.